Read more UNICORN and YETI books!

UNICORN and YETI

Friends Rock

written by
Heather Ayris Burnell

art by
Hazel Quintanilla

ACORN™
SCHOLASTIC INC.

For Jasper — HAB

To Jason, together we rock! — HQ

Text copyright © 2019 by Heather Ayris Burnell
Illustrations copyright © 2019 by Hazel Quintanilla

Library of Congress Cataloging-in-Publication Data

Names: Burnell, Heather Ayris, author. | Quintanilla, Hazel, 1982-, illustrator.
Title: Friends Rock! / by Heather Ayris Burnell ; illustrated by Hazel Quintanilla.
Description: First edition. | New York, NY : Acorn, Scholastic Inc., 2019. |
Series: Unicorn and Yeti ; 3 | Summary: Unicorn and Yeti are still a little new to
the friendship-thing, but they are trying hard to work out
how to share the things they like to do, for instance taking turns on a swing,
or sharing a sparkly rock—or combining the peaches that Unicorn
likes with Yeti's ice cream to make a special treat they can share together.
Identifiers: LCCN 2018053891| ISBN 9781338329070 (pbk.) | ISBN 9781338329087 (hardcover)
Subjects: LCSH: Unicorns—Juvenile fiction. | Yeti—Juvenile fiction. |
Friendship—Juvenile fiction. | Sharing—Juvenile fiction. | Humorous
stories. | CYAC: Unicorns—Fiction. | Yeti—Fiction. |
Friendship—Fiction. | Sharing—Fiction. | Humorous stories. | LCGFT: Humorous fiction.
Classification: LCC PZ7.B92855 Fr 2019 | DDC [E]—dc23 LC record available at https://lccn.loc.gov/2018053891

10 9 8 7 6 5 4 3 2 1   19 20 21 22 23

Printed in China   62

First edition, October 2019

Edited by Katie Carella
Book design by Sarah Dvojack

Table of Contents

Up and Down

Yeti flew in the breeze.

2

And up!

Swinging looks fun.

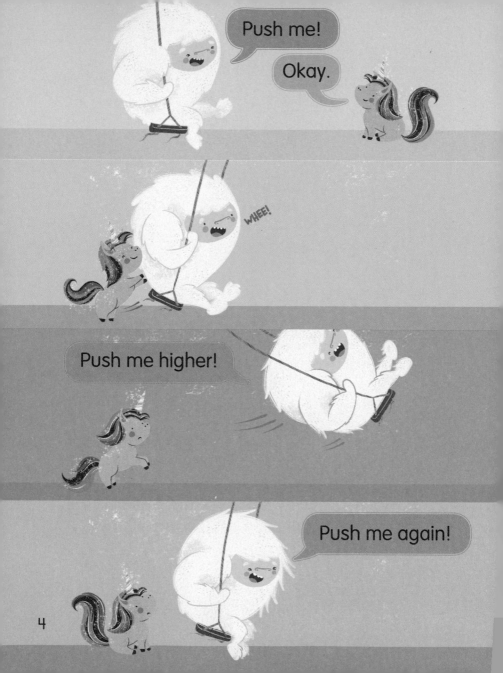

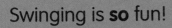

Swinging is **so** fun!

I would like to swing.

You should try it!

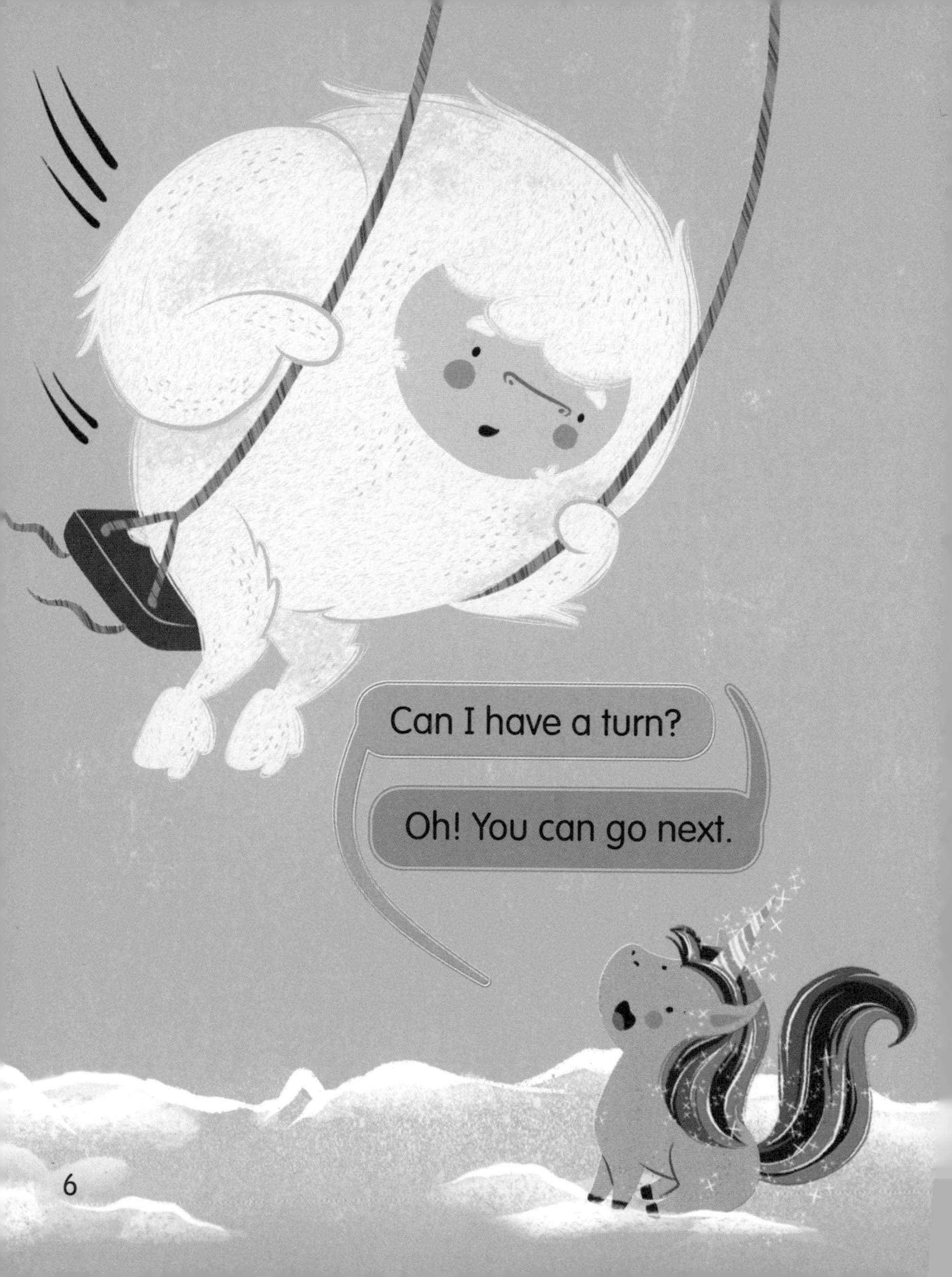
Can I have a turn?
Oh! You can go next.

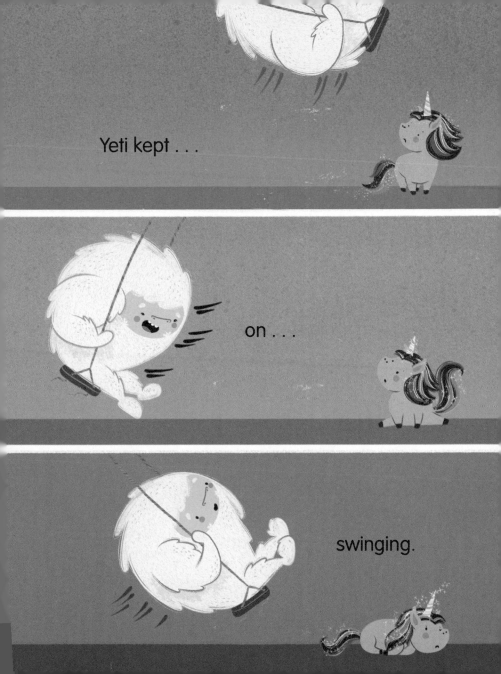

Yeti kept . . .

on . . .

swinging.

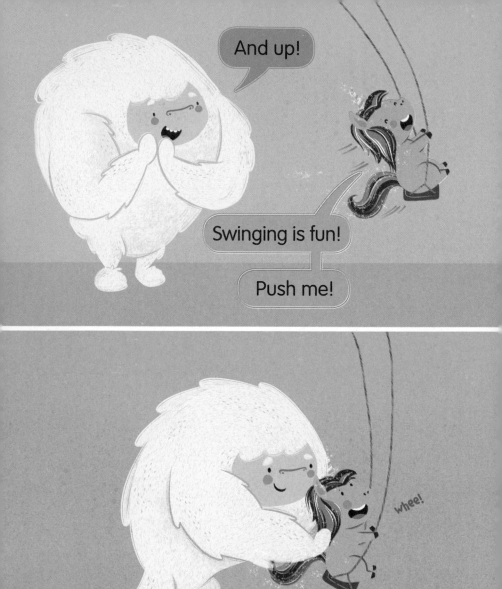

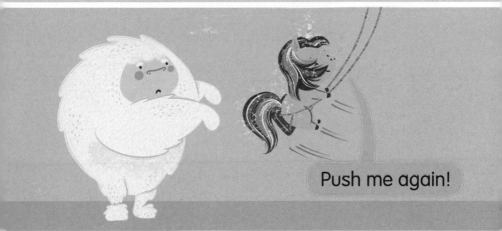

11

You are right.

Swinging is **so** fun!

It is not so fun to be the one doing the pushing.

It was not really fun for me when you were swinging either.

13

Who did you seesaw with?

No one.

A seesaw is made for two. I will show you!

16

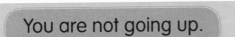

17

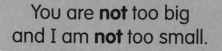

You are **not** too big and I am **not** too small.

You just have to push.

Like this?

19

21

23

A Sparkly Rock

A rock!

It is sparkly.

It is very sparkly.

There is only one rock.
We cannot both have it.
Finders keepers.
But we found it
at the same time.

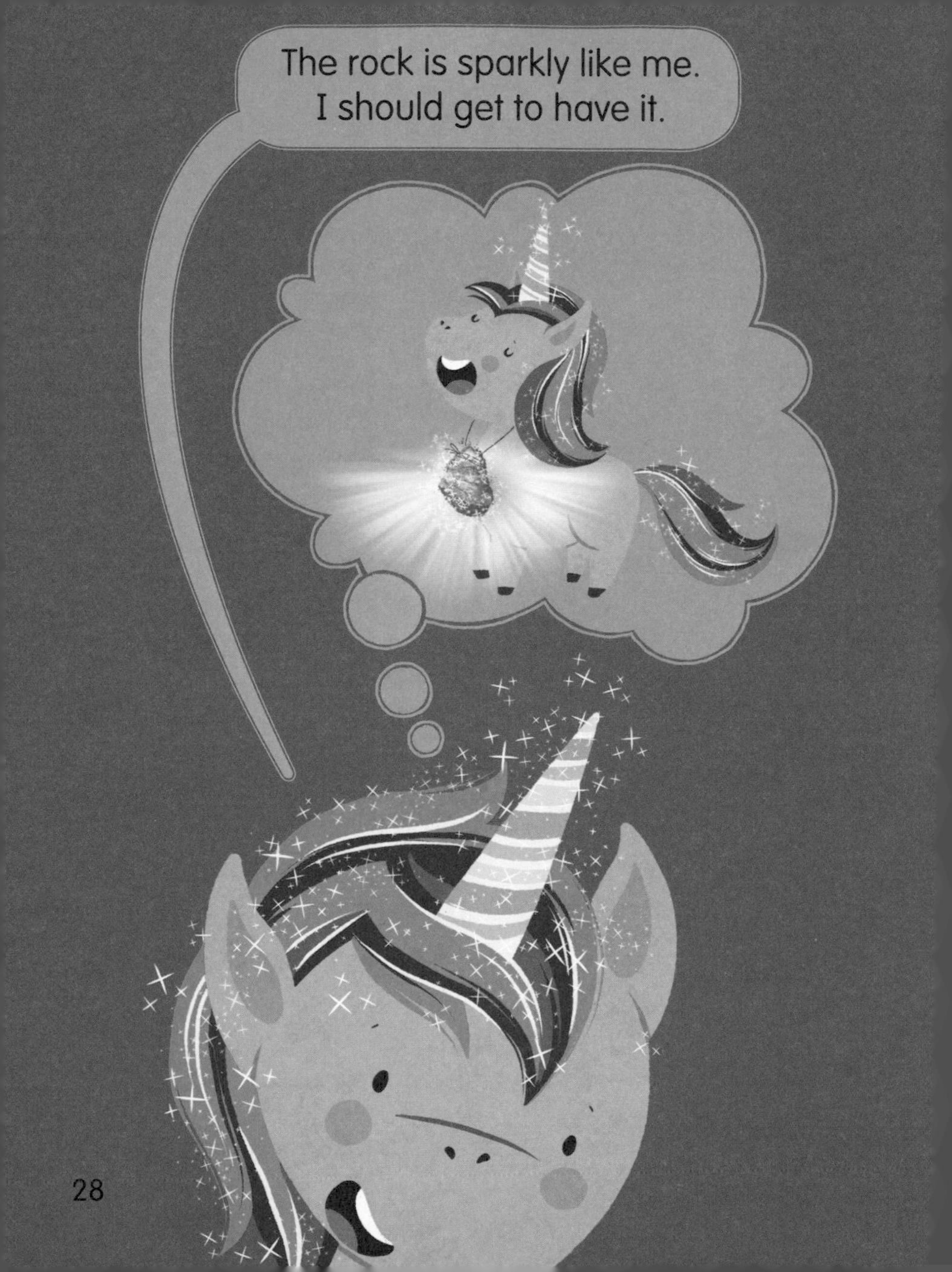
The rock is sparkly like me.
I should get to have it.

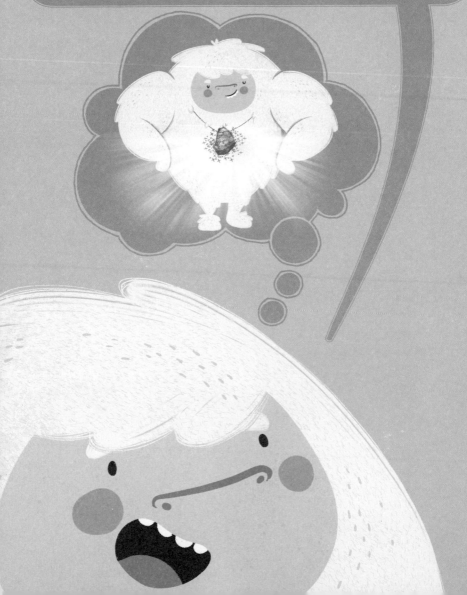

But the rock would make my cloud look fancy.

The rock would make my cave look fancy!

If you put the rock in **your** cave,
then I will not get to see it.

If you put the rock on **your** cloud,
then I will not get to see it.

No fair!

33

Unicorn and Yeti looked for the perfect place
to put the sparkly rock.

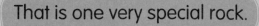

That is one very special rock.

I am glad that it is **ours**.

Me too.

Friends rock!

The Best

Yeti looked at Unicorn.
Unicorn looked at Yeti.

39

Peaches are the best!

Ice cream is the best!

How can **two** things be the best?

I do not know. But I know that peaches are the best.

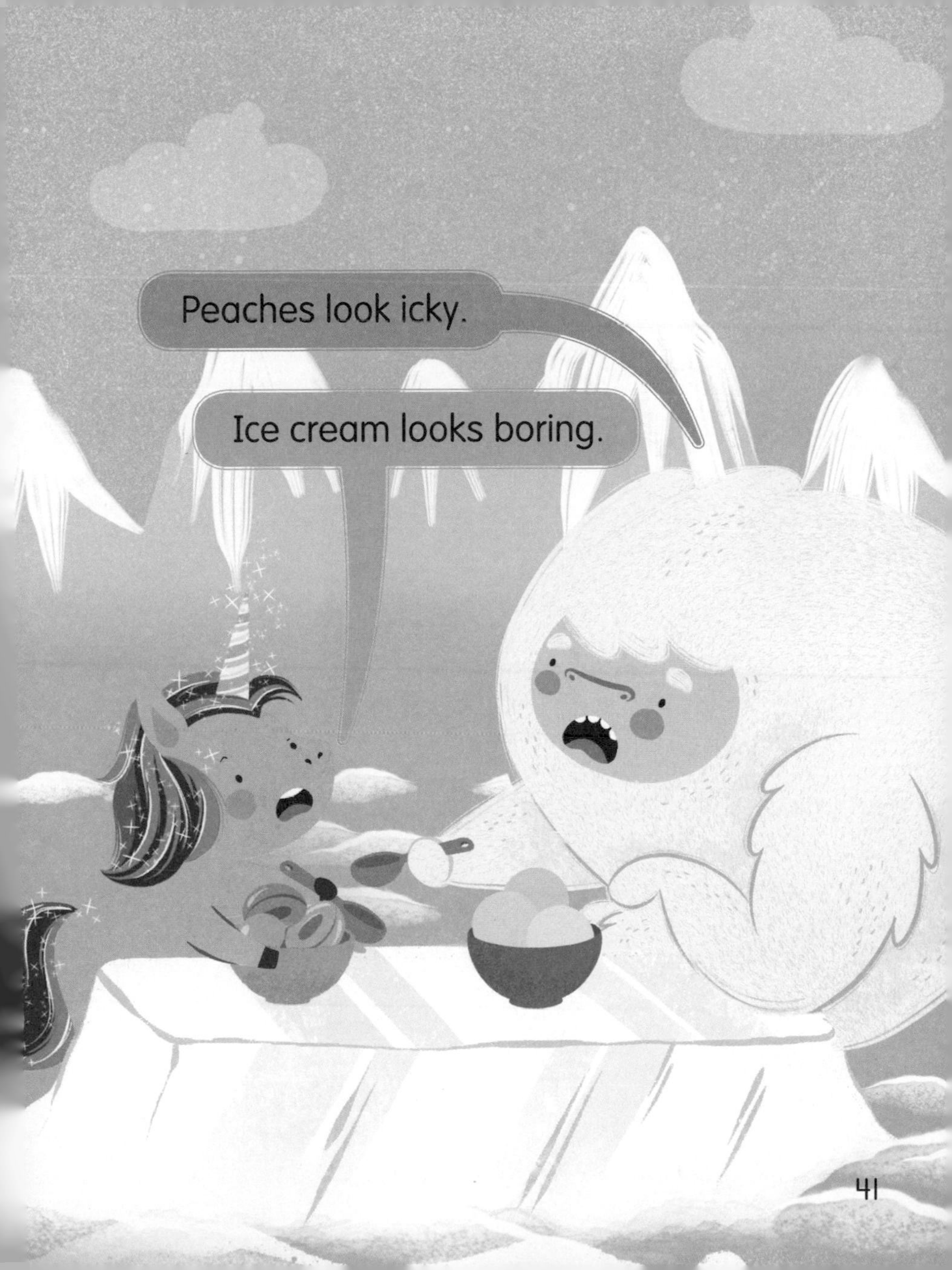
Peaches look icky.
Ice cream looks boring.

Ice cream looks like snow.

It is cold like snow.

I want to try peaches because you say they are the best.

But I do not know if I will like them.

I would try ice cream.

I do not know if I want to share **my** ice cream.

I do not know if I want to share **my** peaches.

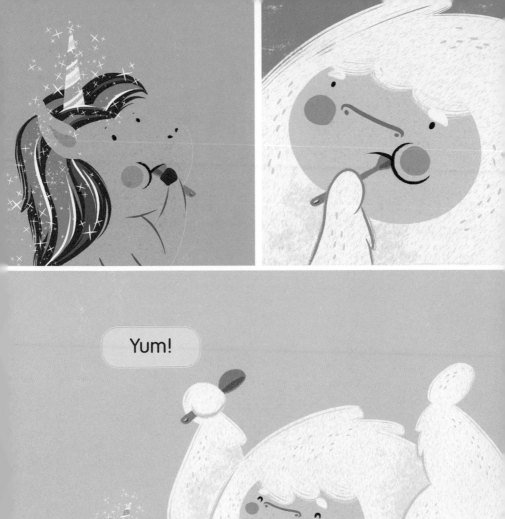

48

But I still like ice cream the best.
Good. Because I still like peaches the best.
HEHE!
HAHA!

Oh no!

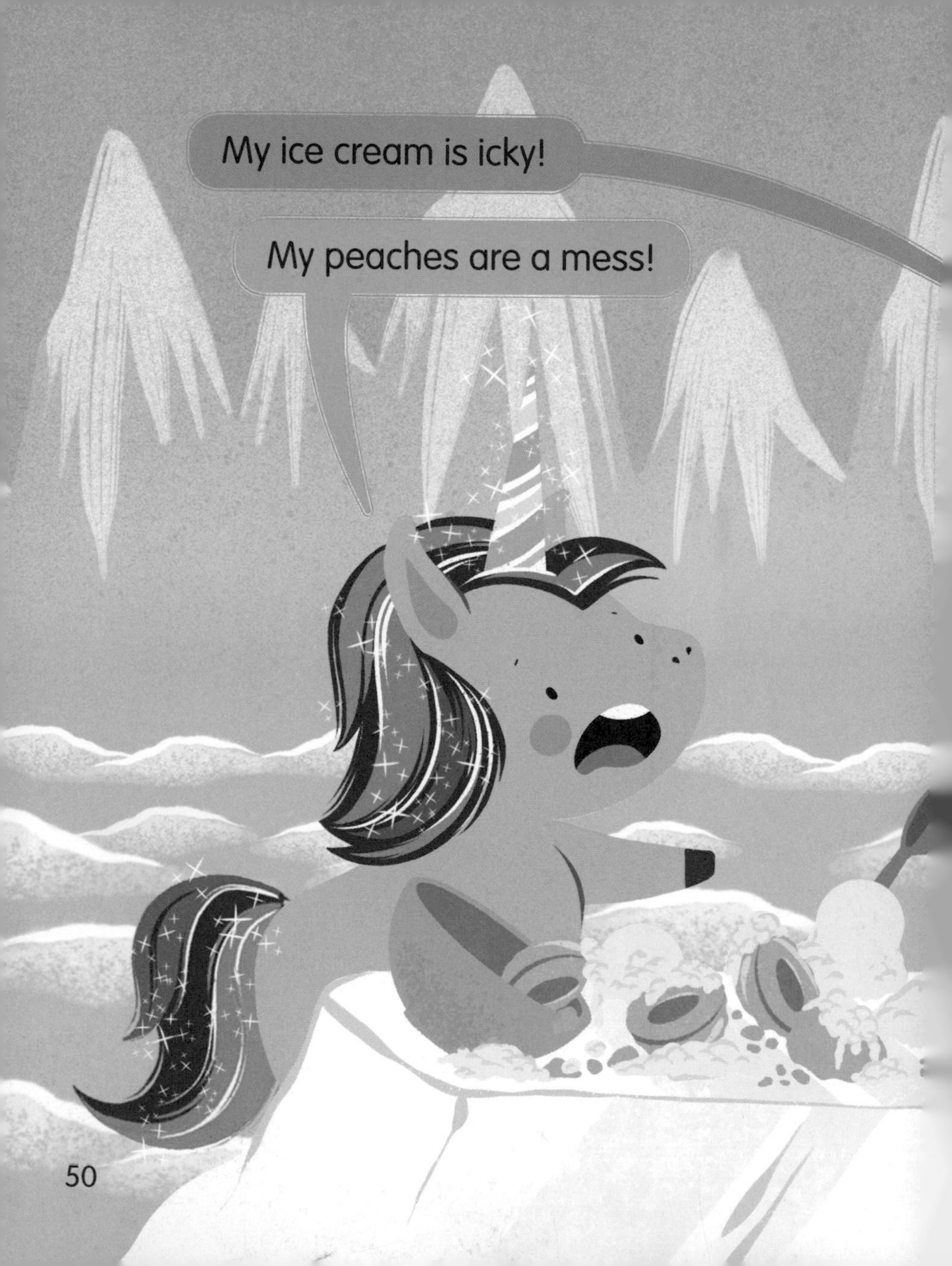
My ice cream is icky!
My peaches are a mess!

53

This is the **best**!

I bet we could make it even better.

How can you make
the **best** better?

55

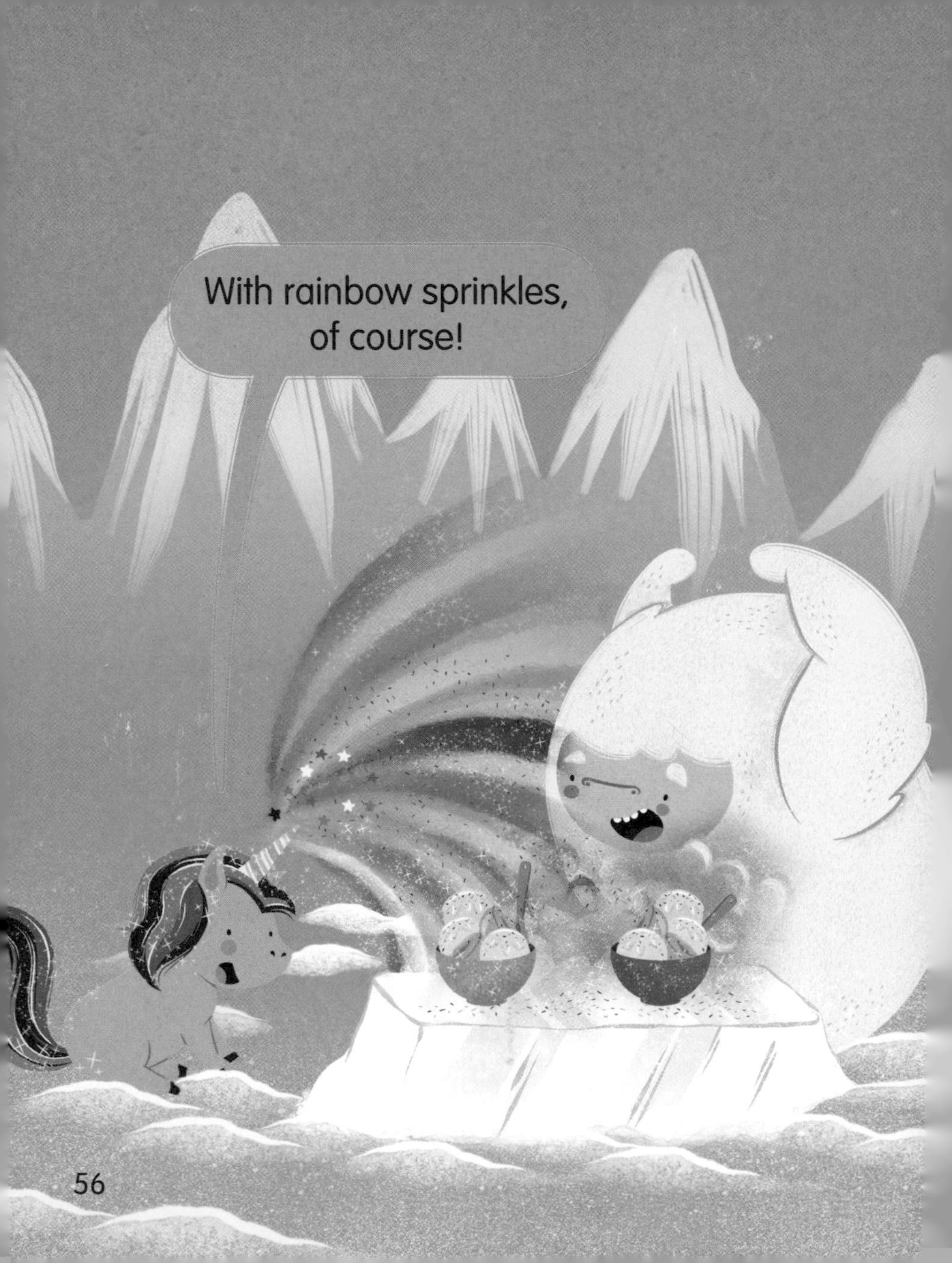
With rainbow sprinkles, of course!

About the Creators

Heather Ayris Burnell lives in Washington state where she loves finding cool rocks. Sometimes the rocks even have sparkles! Heather is a librarian and the author of the Unicorn and Yeti early reader series.

Hazel Quintanilla lives in Guatemala. Hazel always knew she wanted to be an artist. When she was a kid, she carried a pencil and a notebook everywhere.

Hazel illustrates children's books, magazines, and games! And she has a secret: Unicorn and Yeti remind Hazel of her sister and brother. Her siblings are silly, funny, and quirky — just like Unicorn and Yeti!

YOU CAN DRAW PEACHES AND ICE CREAM!

1 Draw a circle lightly with a pencil. (You will erase half of it in the next step!)

2 Draw an oval shape across the middle of the circle. Erase the top of the circle. Now you have a bowl!

3 Draw three small circles inside your bowl. You have three scoops of ice cream!

4 Give your bowl a foot. Add sauce to your ice cream scoops.

5 Add two peach halves into the bowl. Don't forget a spoon.

6 Color in your drawing!

WHAT'S YOUR STORY?

Unicorn and Yeti share their favorite foods.
What is **your** favorite food?
Would you share it with Unicorn and Yeti?
How would it taste mixed with peaches and vanilla ice cream?
Write and draw your story!

scholastic.com/acorn